PUFFIN BOOKS

# The Jealous Giant

# The Jealous Giant

## Kaye Umansky

Illustrated by

## Doffy Weir

PUFFIN BOOKS

PUFFIN BOOKS

Published by the Penguin Group
Penguin Books Ltd, 80 Strand, London WC2R 0RL, England
Penguin Putnam Inc., 375 Hudson Street, New York, New York 10014, USA
Penguin Books Australia Ltd, 250 Camberwell Road, Camberwell, Victoria 3124, Australia
Penguin Books Canada Ltd, 10 Alcorn Avenue, Toronto, Ontario, Canada M4V 3B2
Penguin Books India (P) Ltd, 11 Community Centre, Panchsheel Park, New Delhi – 110 017, India
Penguin Books (NZ) Ltd, Cnr Rosedale and Airborne Roads, Albany, Auckland, New Zealand
Penguin Books (South Africa) (Pty) Ltd, 24 Sturdee Avenue, Rosebank 2196, South Africa

Penguin Books Ltd, Registered Offices: 80 Strand, London WC2R 0RL, England

www.penguin.com

First published by Hamish Hamilton Ltd 1997
Published in Puffin Books 1998
9 10 8

Printed and bound in China by Leo Paper Products Ltd

0–140–38840–0

Giant Waldo was really very fond of his
next-door neighbour. Her name was Heavy
Hetty, and she had everything a giant
needed in a girl friend. Big biceps. Massive
muscles. A kind heart. And she could cook,
too. This suited Waldo, who tended to live
on burnt toast and things out of packets
when left to his own devices.

Waldo got used to having his supper round at Hetty's every night. Huge roast dinners with all the trimmings, followed by apple crumble and custard. On Saturdays, there were little minty chocolates as well.

Hetty's meals didn't come out of packets. She bought everything fresh and spent hours chopping and peeling. And all this after a hard day's work!

Hetty was a wrestler. Her name appeared on posters all over the country. The posters said:

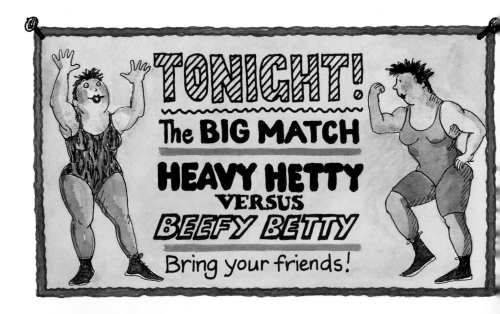

**TONIGHT!**
The **BIG MATCH**
**HEAVY HETTY**
*VERSUS*
*BEEFY BETTY*
Bring your friends!

Hetty's wrestling career was very successful and she won a lot of cups. But she had to work hard to stay at the top. It was very important to keep fit. She jogged and skipped and worked out. And then she went shopping, came home, tidied the cave, washed her hair and cooked supper for Waldo.

Waldo didn't work. He usually got up late. After a leisurely breakfast of burnt toast, he would then collapse into a hammock and spend the rest of the day thinking about what he might get for supper. Sometimes he would even stroll down to the shop for the paper. Then he would return to his cave and snooze over the crossword puzzle.

Finally, at seven o'clock sharp, roused by the delicious smells wafting from the cave next door, he would hot foot it round to Hetty's, where another glorious feast awaited.

Waldo got so used to Hetty's meals that he started popping little notes in with suggestions as to what he would like.

Dear Het,
Any chance of chips for a change? And don't put so much salt in the broccoli. See you tonight.
Love, Waldo.

One night, Waldo was just spooning up the last mouthful of pudding, when Hetty gave a little sigh. Waldo looked across the table and noticed she hadn't touched her supper.

"What's up, Het?" asked Waldo.

"I lost another match last night," said Hetty. "Betty beat me, two falls to one.

That's the third time in a row. I think I'm
working too hard. I keep falling asleep in
the middle of a bout. I think it's all the
shopping and cooking. Do you think we
could go out to eat one night for a change?"

"Oh, we don't want to do *that*!" cried
Waldo, shocked. "We don't want to eat *out*.
Eating out's expensive. Anyway, I like good
home cooking. Any more of that pudding?"

Next evening, when Waldo went round to
Hetty's, he found a short note on the front
boulder. It said:

Waldo,
Gone out to
meet my new
coach.
Sorry about
supper.
Hetty

"Well I never! That's a bit much," said
Waldo. And he went back to his own cave
and sulked.

The sun was high when he awoke next
morning. Without even stopping to burn
himself some toast, he went right round to
Hetty's cave.

Much to his surprise,
Hetty had company.

The visitor had big,
rippling muscles that
bulged all over the place
and a lot of shiny
white teeth. Waldo
disliked him
on sight.

"Oh, hello, Waldo,"
said Hetty. "This is Ed,
my new coach."

"Hi!" said Ed's teeth.

"Umf," grunted Waldo.

"We're just off training,"
explained Hetty. "I expect
I shall be out most of the day."

"But what about my supper?"
asked Waldo.

"I'm not cooking tonight. Ed and I are going out for a salad," said Hetty. "He wants to discuss my footwork. 'Bye."

Waldo watched them jog briskly into the distance. Then he went home to kick the wall.

That night, Waldo watched from behind
the curtains. He saw Ed arrive with a
bunch of pansies. He saw Hetty emerge,
looking very glamorous in her best dress
and dangly earrings. He saw them walk
down the mountain together, chatting away
about wrestling.

Hetty got home late that night. Waldo
knew, because he waited up and spied on
her through his window.

"I don't like that Ed," Waldo told Hetty when he saw her next day.

"Don't be silly, Waldo," said Hetty. "Why ever not?"

"I don't trust his teeth," said Waldo.

"Why, Waldo!" said Hetty. "I do believe you're jealous."

"No I'm not," growled Waldo. "I'm hungry, though," he added.

"You'd best cook yourself some supper, then," said Hetty tartly.

"I will," said Waldo. "Cooking's easy-peasy."

And he stomped crossly back to his cave.

From then on, there were no more cosy suppers. Hetty spent every day training and every evening out with Ed. She never seemed to be in.

After a week of burnt toast and things from packets, Waldo stuck a note on Hetty's boulder. It said:

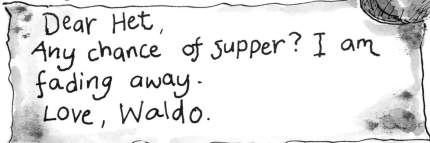

Dear Het,
Any chance of supper? I am fading away.
Love, Waldo.

But she didn't reply.

Waldo decided something must be done. He set his alarm clock really early one morning, got up, took his basket and went out shopping. When he returned, he put on an apron and got to work. He chopped and peeled and grated and sliced. He measured and tasted and simmered and fried. He

used every pot he possessed, and made a
shocking mess. But, to his great triumph,
he finally had a big pot of stew bubbling
away on the stove and a cake in the oven.

After he had cleaned up, which took
ages, Waldo had a wash, combed his beard
and changed his socks. Then he laid the
table with a white cloth and put a bunch of
daisies in a jam jar. It looked very nice.

Then he went round to Hetty's and stuck
another note on her boulder. This one said:

Dear Het,
Supper tonight at my place.
Seven o'clock sharp.
PLEASE come.
Love, Waldo.

Then, feeling very pleased with himself,
he went back home to put his feet up for ten
minutes, worn out with all the
unaccustomed hard work.

Several hours later, Waldo woke to find the cave full of thick, black smoke! With a choking cry, he groped his way to the oven, where his lovely stew had quite boiled away, leaving a thick, gloppy, tar-like mess in the bottom of the pan. And as for his cake – well. It was a charred, smoking ruin.

Gasping for air, he staggered from the cave – and ran slap bang into Hetty! She was all dressed up, with her earrings and everything. For once, there was no sign of Ed.

"Hello, Waldo," said Hetty. "I got your note. I was just coming round for supper."

Waldo said nothing. He was coughing too badly. Hetty patted him on the back.

"Looks like you've had a bit of a disaster," she said, with a little smile.

"I have," admitted Waldo. "It's hard work, this cooking business."

"I know," said Hetty.

"I don't know how you do it all the time," said Waldo. "On top of a full-time career. By the way – how is your career?"

"It's going very well, thank you, Waldo," said Hetty cheerfully. "I've beaten Beefy Betty three times in a row. I'm right back up to my peak of fitness again. Thanks to Ed."

"Mmmm," said Waldo. And added casually, "Where is Ed, tonight, by the way?"

"Coaching Betty," said Hetty. "She needs it more than me."

"Good," said Waldo. Then, because he couldn't help it, he burst out:

"Oh, Het. Where have you been these last few weeks? I've missed you!"

"Missed my cooking, more like," said Hetty.

"No. Well, yes. But most of all I've missed you."

"Really, Waldo?"

"Really."

"Well, that's nice," said Hetty. "Because I've missed you too."

Fireworks! Flowers! Twittering birds and a big explosion of hearts!

"I tell you what, Het," said Waldo, wiping his streaming eyes. "Let's go out to dinner, eh? My treat. They do a lovely special down at the Three Ogres. Agreed?"

"Agreed," said Hetty,
giving him a big  hug.

And if you want to know what they ate, here it is. Hetty had a sensible salad with a glass of carrot juice. And Waldo had sausages, beans, mushrooms, mashed potatoes and broccoli, followed by apple crumble and custard.

And lots of little minty chocolates to finish with.

*Also available in First Young Puffin*


## PINK FOR POLAR BEAR
### Valerie Solís

All the other polar bears tease Nanook because she is
pink. Then she makes some new friends who help her
discover her own very special talent . . .


## THE POCKET ELEPHANT
### Catherine Sefton

Mary has a little elephant who lives in a special
pocket in her cardigan. One day Mary takes
her elephant to school – and the elephant discovers
a big world outside the pocket!

## RITA THE RESCUER
### Hilda Offen

Rita Potter, the youngest of the Potter children, is a
very special person. When a mystery parcel arrives at
her house, Rita finds a Rescuer's outfit inside and races
off to perform some very daring rescues.